HOW IT FEELS
TO BE A BOAT

HOW IT FEELS

TO BE A BOAT

Written and illustrated by **James Kwan**

HOUGHTON MIFFLIN HARCOURT

Boston   New York

To Chloe: Welcome to Earth!

www.hmhco.com

The text of this book is set in Amasis MT Std.
The illustrations are made from several layers of graphite renderings and watercolor textures, which are combined and colored digitally.

Library of Congress Cataloging-in-Publication Data is on file.

ISBN 978-0-544-71533-2

Manufactured in China
SCP 10 9 8 7 6 5 4 3 2 1
4500647821

You are a boat.

Ahoy, ahoy!
Raise your crooked anchor and head out to sea,
as your foghorn howls and barnacles tickle your bottom.

You are a boat!
With your squirmy corridors that twist inside,
your levers and pulleys that flex your strong muscles,
and your furnace-heart that pushes you forward,
tearing the sea in two.

And look—rooms upon rooms in your belly!
So how does it feel to be a boat?
How does it feel to hold everyone in your belly-rooms?

Inside,
your halls fill with the sweet doughy smell
of the Chef's delicious treats.

Your rooms echo as the Big Brass Band plays
your favorite doot-doot tune,
and Daniel sings along: *lee lee lee doo*.

Deeper down, your belly rumbles as
the Octopus's gadgets hum and shake,

while the Superhero waits
quietly by his phone.

By your furnace-heart Bill and June keep warm,
painting each other's toes.

In your belly everyone gets along,

but sometimes they fight.

When they yell your belly aches,
your heart shrinks, and your rooms shiver.

You are strong, but sometimes you tremble.

Still, onward you go!
Up and over the salty sea once again,
sputtering millions of baby bubbles behind you.

So where are you going?
Where are you taking everyone?

The Chef wants to go east—
she's late for a birthday party—

but the Octopus wants to go
way south, back to her bed.

The Big Brass Band wants to go northwest to play a song for their mothers.

The Superhero needs to go
southeast immediately!

Daniel wants to go there too,
but Bill and June don't want
to go anywhere.

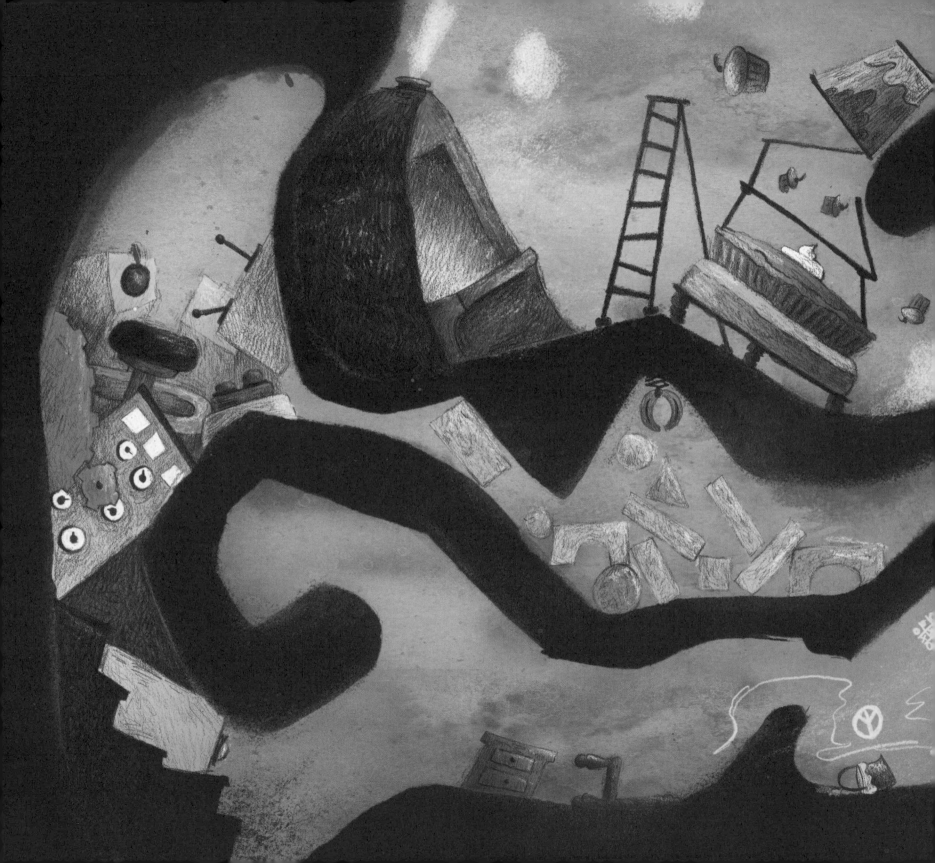

Inside, you writhe and squirm.
They yell and you feel yourself tremble.

They jerk the wheel left and you jerk left,

and they spin right and you spin right.

No, no, no—a little up and a little down.

Northeast! Southwest!

Watch out up ahead!

The wheel spins and spins

and you . . .

Remember, you are strong,

and piece by crooked piece you are made.

From inside your belly you smell a delicious thing
and hear your favorite doot-doot tune
and feel everyone singing and moving together:
lee lee lee doo.

You are crooked, but you are strong.

You are a boat.

Ahoy, ahoy!